Shades and Silver

Scions and Shadows

Dax Murray

Kraken Collective

DAX MURRAY

SHADES AND SILVER

ISLES OF THE
ÁSTFRÍÐUR
KIRRIOV
KRYLLYA
SORTALOVA
AHNLISEN
LINEA
HIJAR RIVER
ALA
GALIV
MERIDA
R-
WHICK
BERACH
VALENCIA
GARCEL
LAOCRE
MADRILLIA
HERN
EOI
SALIH UL
FAYN
TAERN'S
KEEP
SANRAS
CLARE

SEKRISTAL
ETOKRASA
RYNNIQ
NIMES
ANDELLA RIVER
LYONE
Lake Ixela
JANEUQ
ALLEGHENAIE RIVER
CYGNE
OUISNE
HAUT VEN
IRI
AVON RIVER
IZMYRI
ERID
IVAH
ZAPPAHRIA
SUA
ERZURUMEI
IJ
MASYAF
ESIRI
ARRINHU
I
ANTALYZA
SHA DHABU

this one is for me

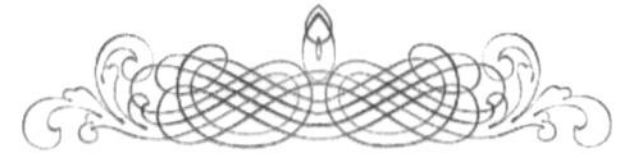

SHADES

T HE SUN WAS JUST cresting the horizon, and the western-facing windows caught every ray, a shining sword slicing through the night. But it could not cut through the dark that was overtaking Britt's vision as it went wobbly, and then it went black. They spread their arms out, looking for something they could lean on, something that could support their weight while they could not do so for themselves. Their legs were unsteady, tingling, and unable to provide a center of balance. Britt swore. They would never get used to this. Their hand found the rough wall, and they leaned into it, closing their eyes and waiting for the vertigo to pass.

They took a breath, and opened their eyes again, focusing on their tungsten-tinted hands pressed against the elm walls. I've got this. I'm okay. They took a tentative step, and then another. Each step felt steadier than the previous. The world stopped spinning around them, and they sighed, relieved that the episode had been relatively short. They'd been hoping that today would have been one of their good days. No such luck.

Britt took one more deep breath and then entered the kitchen. Alva and Coraline were already awake and busy in the kitchen. Their caregivers were an odd pair, Alva was a fellow *Ástfríður*, while Coraline was a mortal spellweaver from Fayn, but they made it work. Alva was seated at the table, thumbing through a worn cookbook, their matte silver skin glowing the color of the moon on a sheet of ice and the morning light illuminating the copper ahnhörn that adorned their head.

"Good morning, Britt! Big day today!" Coraline said.

Britt tried to parse the words, but the pain in their head was insistent, crowding out everything else. They knew they were supposed to respond, but they forgot the words.

It was a day like any other, and yet it was the last of such days; their last morning as a tonå, an Ástfríður who had not yet made their ahnhörn, someone who had not yet chosen their path in life. Britt sat down next to Alva, reaching for the bone knife and peeling an apple. It seemed so unfair that today would start like this.

The clang of the *klämta* ricocheted around their kitchen. The sound of the bell was like a bone pick hammering at their head—another residual effect, the afterimage of their accident. But the Veil would not cease their traditions just because they had fallen and hit their head and could no longer bear sound, touch, or light, in any large quantities. And so the *Sång* rang the bell and announced the arrival of another *spädba*—tiny and sleeping at the base of the Tree—in the only way they knew how. Britt had found this comforting once, but the joyous sound of a soul returning could now leave them in bed for days with a brutal headache. "I wonder," Coraline said, looking up from the stone pot she had over the brick stove. "I had a dream about Arvid last night."

"It's possible. That would be nice if they were back," Alva said. "What about this?" Alva pointed to the book and looked up at Coraline.

"I think that would be perfect."

"Britt, do you want *semla* for your celebration tonight?"

"Umm, sure." The doughy and sweet dessert, filled with a thick and sugary cream, a favorite of both Britt's and Alva's, was saved for special occasions. Today qualified, but the thought of a celebration after *Väljahnhörn* was a burning pit in their stomach. A celebration afterward meant that they had to go, decide who they would be, and how they would wander through this world. Britt reached for the small bracelet that they had been wearing on the day they were found by the *Sång* as a *spädba* at the Tree. They spun the cool copper around their wrist. The bracelet was a constant presence: sometimes it felt incredibly familiar, sometimes uncomfortably foreign.

It would be easy to pick copper; a metal of creativity, of passion. It would be easy to settle into a path they knew that they had walked at least once before, even though they could not remember that life. It would be straightforward: melt the bracelet down and reforge it as their new ahnhörn, the beautiful circlet and affixed horn that every adult Ástfríður wore upon their heads. No one would think it odd for Britt to pick the same path in this life as they had chosen in their previous life. Many people reforged their ahnhörn into a bracelet, using the flames that consumed them before their rebirth at the base of the Tree. It was supposed to be reminder of their past.

They had no clue how they'd lived as copper in their previous life. Their accident had left them unable to partake in many of the creative joys of life. Was that path now closed to them? And yet, *Väljahnhörn* was also an opportunity to choose differently. To cast off the remains of the previous life, return that metal to the Mother, and draw up new. Alva was copper, and had, for as far back as the records stated, always chosen to remain copper. The *Sång* was gold and platinum, and their *ahnhörn* was a beautiful swirl of the two metals spiraling around each other before blending into one at the sharp point. Tungsten, bronze, pewter—all had meaning and history. Some elected, like the *Sång*, to entwine two or more together. Others had combined two into one, mixing gold and copper for a rose-tinted hue.

But Britt did not have this history of their past lives to consult; they were *tvära*, born into a clan they had not been in before. There was no record of them here, no one who remembered them. No one who could tell them stories of who they had been, what they had loved, what inspired them. Being *tvära* was uncommon, but it was nothing to be ashamed of. But here they were, a *tvära* about to choose an *ahnhörn*, about to leave behind their *tonå* years and take their place as an adult of the Veil, and they did not feel they had the information they needed. Had other *tvära* felt this lost? This ill-equipped? Britt was torn. If only they had even a glimmer of their history, they might be able to make a choice. The *Sång* said tvära were *tvära* for a reason; forsaking the past was a choice. But would Britt's past self have chosen this path if they'd known what Britt's future looked like?

"Are you ready to go?" Coraline asked, louder than she normally might have. Britt got the impression that this was not the first time she had asked.

"Oh, I'm ready. Sorry."

The second their foot touched the bare earth outside their home of wood and thatch, they felt the metal singing, some of it waiting just beneath the surface, so much of it deeper in the earth. If they wanted, they knew they could pluck that metal from the earth, melt it with a thought, and shape it as they pleased with a breath of air and their will. After all, the birthright of every *Ástfríður* was to know each metal in the earth, command it, bend it to their desires. Every *Ástfríður* learned how to navigate the world by following the blood of the Gods: copper for the Creator, titanium for the Trickster, silver for the Seer, each underground river of divinity guiding the *Ástfríður* on whatever road they chose. Britt followed the pull of the metals, guided by the veins of the Gods.

The flow of copper led them to the Tree, nearly as bright as the stars in the night but more devastatingly beautiful, for it was immortal, metal already born. It had stood as long as the people of the Veil could re-member, as constant as the break of dawn, as precious as family. The roots of copper linked to everything in the domain of the Veil. Its branches never tarnished, and each autumn, the the *Sång* collected the silver, gold, and platinum leaves as they fell, saving them so that every ahnhörnu could forge them into offerings to the Gods, trinkets on private altars, jewelry worn only on holy days. After today, Britt would be ahnhörnu. A full member of the Veil, in whatever capacity they chose.

"Good morning, Britt." The *Sång* smiled, their arms clasped in front of them, a long tunic made of gold clinging to their body. They wore their ceremonial jewelry; any day a *tonå* went through *Väljahnhörn* was a holy day, just as any day a *spädba* appeared at dawn at the foot of the Tree. Twice blessed, then.

"Good morning, Caregiver."

"Seventeen years ago you appeared here, at the base of this Tree."

Britt swallowed and nodded.

"You are *tvära*. Your soul has never lived beneath these leaves before. Some part of you chose to come here. And today, you will choose what to do now that you are here."

Unable to find words, Britt nodded again. Aphasia; another afterimage.

"You will find many things during *Väljahnhörn*. But, you do not have to bring back everything that you find. Are you ready?"

"No, but." Britt stumbled. "I mean—"

"No one ever is."

Britt wondered if the *Sång* was saying that to be encouraging or if it was really true.

"I'm afraid..."

The *Sång* waited.

"What if I can't, what if I'm unable to or I get sick or...?"

"Each *Väljahnhörn* is unique to the *Ástfríður* undertaking it."

This didn't quite quell the fear in Britt. "Okay." They took a deep breath. "I'm as ready as I'll ever be." The Sång walked ahead, and Britt tried to follow, clinging to the copper in the ground and the iron in the *Sång's* blood.

In silence, they walked until they were at the outskirts of the Veil. Britt felt the last reaches of the Tree's roots fall behind them. They'd never gone past the roots before. But the *Sång* kept walking, so Britt kept following.

Britt stumbled as a wave of vertigo washed over them. People, attempting to diagnose the condition, would often ask if it felt like they were spinning or if the world was spinning. Britt tried to figure it out every time this happened, but it always felt like both. *Not now, not now, please.*

It was a short eternity until Britt felt capable of proceeding. The *Sång* had paused and was looking back at them with concern, but obvious restraint. Britt respected this companionable distance. Being so vulnerable, so incapable, was one thing, but being like that in front of other people was embarrassing.

"I'm all right now. We can move on."

"But we have arrived."

From some well-concealed pocket, the *Sång* pulled out a canvas flask and handed it to Britt. It felt strange in their hands—lighter than it should have been. They pulled the stopper and drank it.

The liquid was heavy. It was thick and warm and full of iron. Each drop made itself known as it washed down their throat, slow as honey and thick as cream.

"Come back to the Veil when you are ready, with whatever you want to bring back with you." The *Sång* passed Britt, moving as if they were not tied to the ground, as if they could ask the trees to move out of their way.

"Wait! What am I supposed to do?" But the *Sång* did not turn around, did not acknowledge them. Britt slumped to the forest floor and picked up twigs and other detritus from long-gone ant empires and bird colonies. One by one, they flung the former building materials as far as they could. Sometimes they struck trees, rustled leaves, and disturbed sleeping squirrels.

"At this rate, your celebratory dinner and dessert will be cold when you finally arrive home."

Britt screamed, springing to their feet and scanning the forest for the source of the voice. Behind them, they saw an elderly *Ástfríður* approaching, a cane of bone and wood in their left hand, robes trailing behind them. The sun made their coppery skin glow like the smoldering embers in a hearth. Britt tried to slow their heart, taking deep breaths and holding them in for a count before releasing them. The elder continued, unperturbed by Britt's scream.

"I didn't mean to frighten you," they said to Britt.

"It's fine, Elder. Are you lost?"

"I'm coming to visit you."

"Oh?" Britt reevaluated the elderly *Ástfriður*, but didn't recognize them. "Now isn't the best of times. I'm rather busy."

"Is that so?" The elderly *Ástfriður* was now close enough that Britt could make out their *ahnhörn*. They sensed the copper in it, warm and familiar, but old. The metal had left the earth centuries ago, and it had been shaped and reshaped many times. "What are you so busy doing?"

"I think, whatever it is one should do during their *Väljahnhörn*." Britt was trying to be polite but got the distinct impression they were being baited.

"It looks like a bunch of nothing to me."

"Well, I'm not quite sure what I'm supposed to do, but I would like to keep trying."

With practiced grace, the elder readjusted their diaphanous robes and sat on the forest floor across from Britt, placing their cane across their lap. "Would you like me to help you?" The question was not mocking or condescending, it held the weight of someone who was making a promise. But Britt was not sure they wanted to know what that promise was.

Britt settled on asking, "Is that allowed? I thought I was supposed to do this on my own."

The elder leaned forward, mischief lighting up in their eyes. "Oh, you are certainly allowed to accept my help."

Britt felt the ground beneath them shift. They set their hands on the ground and leaned forward, unsure if this was another episode of pain and disorientation or if there really was a seismic shift. Their eyes flickered upward, trying to gauge the reaction of the elder. But the elder seemed unmoved. And then it clicked.

"I see. I'm still alone here," Britt said to this unexpected apparition of their past.

"Technically, yes." There was kindness in their voice.

Silence stretched between them, the shade watching as Britt attempted to compose themself. When Britt finally sat up, meeting the shade's eyes, the shade asked, "Are you ill?"

"There was an accident," Britt said, unsure of how much detail to give. "I haven't really been the same since."

"I'm listening," the shade said.

"I don't remember what happened, really. One minute I was at home, upstairs in my bed, and the next I was sprawled at the base of the stairs. I'm not sure how long I was there."

"You are a different being now, you feel?"

"I guess. My caregivers have tried to help, but it's been two years and I still hurt every day. It's as though it's always autumn, and I see the leaves falling away from me but I know that they won't grow back come spring."

The elder sat back, empathy etched in their face.

"I don't know, I'm supposed to make my *ahnhörn*, but I'm *tvära*. I have no record of my past lives and no idea how to shape this one." Britt stood up a little too quickly.

"It's your choice. Everything during *Väljahnhörn* is your choice."

Answers. The questions Britt only dared to ask into the dark of a moonless night, the questions they flung to the stars and hoped would burn to ash, unanswered but no longer plaguing them. The questions they needed to ask but feared the answers to. Questions that made them shake with shame for even daring to put words to them. They shouldn't be questioning their past self's choice to be *tvära*. *Tvära* were supposed to accept the choices of their past selves.

And yet.

Why. "Who were you?"

"A bard, a storyteller, a wanderer," the shade started, and their voice took on a deliberateness, the weightiness of simple fact plainly spoken. "A musician, a dancer, a lover of many but partner to few. Too radical for those of the Mountain-at-Dawn."

"And your *ahnhörn*?"

"Made from the bracelet around my wrist when I was found as a *spädba* at the edge of the Silver Lake."

The words wrapped around Britt, but their sluggish brain could not process them. Could not, but also would not. They did not want to realize that this past gave no guidance for the future. "I can't even watch people dance now because it makes me too dizzy. Certain pitches give me headaches that force me to hide in a dark and quiet room. I'm afraid of even going on long walks alone."

They had been right to fear these answers, these pasts they could not remember and had no record of, these happier days they could not even re-experience in memories. Why had they asked, even in a roundabout fashion? They had no claim on the copper bracelet on their wrist. They could not carry this past with them. They had no right to that past now that they were unable to embrace, with full zeal, what it meant to be copper. They could not choose again the copper of music, dance, oration—a life of happiness and weightless wandering.

They spun the copper around on their wrist. If not copper, then what? Maybe pewter or bronze. Quiet metals: pewter, the cool quiet of a solitary and philosophical life, and bronze, the warm quiet life of healing others or working in the temple—and both composed somewhat of copper, a small concession to the past. Britt focused on the earth and began speaking the language of the Gods, seeking out the veins of these metals. They were not close, but they felt confident that they could call these metals to them, at least in the small amounts they would need to craft a simple *ahnhörn*. They were lucky, in a way, that they were not from the Mountain-at-Dawn. That clan would have frowned on them calling more metals to compare or to blend. They were far more conservative about their metal use than the Veil.

But. Would they have had an accident if they'd been reborn again at Mountain-at-Dawn? If they never had the accident, would they be—?

"There's no way to know that, but we chose the Veil for a reason," the elder answered.

"And the life before—?"

"I did not ask at my *Väljahnhörn*. And I was a *tvära* in the Mountain-at-Dawn."

A few years earlier, on a day bright and clear, the sky had started getting dark far too soon. The sun still stood at attention above them, but it seemed to grow darker. Insects that slept during the day woke up, and animals that grazed during the day began looking for a place to sleep. Bats launched into the growing darkness and birds flew from it. For five long minutes, night overtook day and the sun disappeared from the sky. Stars shone but no moon could be seen accompanying them. That period of complete chaos, when all knowledge and truth seemed to be so reversed, had been the scariest and most disorienting few moments of Britt's life.

But that feeling of the world being turned upside down was eclipsed by this moment. Britt had been holding out hope that their *Väljahnhörn* would uncover some knowledge deep inside of them that hadn't gotten lost during their rebirth. That hope had been like a ciphered codex, the answers there but obfuscated. But now they found the decryption page turning to ash in their hands.

This whole process was unfair. The accident was unfair. They had lost control of their body, their history, and their future. They had imagined that learning about their past would point the way forward, allowing them to follow a path of a different choosing. They'd come here both wanting to choose copper again and hoping for a reason to choose differently.

But the emptiness inside as they realized that they were without a choice shocked them. Had they really been so attached to copper that the denial of it had opened a gaping wound in their heart?

"Britt."

They hadn't felt this hollow since the week immediately after the fall. That week when time didn't make sense and they couldn't order their memories chronologically; when they were hiding from all stimulation. Touch, smell, or sight—it was all too overwhelming.

"Britt."

They had feared they could never enjoy anything ever again, their body had forgotten how to sleep and even Coraline's tea did not help. They secluded themself under the quilts and blankets and did not leave their room unless they had to.

"Britt! Britt. Stop." Britt had been staring at a pebble on the ground while they spiraled into the drowning dark. They jerked their head up to look at the elderly *ahnhörnu* in front of them. The shade of their former life smiled at them, a smile that crept into their eyes and offered comfort. "Tell me, what do you think being copper means?"

Britt thought back to the morning when Alva and Coraline had hoped that the tiny *spädba* at the base of the Tree was Arvid reborn. "There was someone who took the journey three years ago. I remember there was a festival. It was early spring and we were dancing, their golden skin shimmered like a bonfire on a full-moon night. Their silver *ahnhörn* reflected the reds and oranges of the torches, giving the illusion that Arvid had chosen copper."

Britt told their shade that Arvid was a blur of passion and energy; their joy was a warm summer afternoon, and their laughter was the wind in the chimes. About the way that Arvid seemed to see the future every dawn and greeted it with jubilance, that was the silver in them—seeing the future so brightly. How Arvid had taught Britt to make different instruments yell, whisper, or weep. Britt explained that they had learned the art of choreographed chaos from Arvid, dancing with anyone who would laugh along until the moon had set and dawn had overtaken the horizon.

"Arvid was silver, but still, it is their face I usually see when I think of copper. I know it doesn't make sense."

"Copper is more than aesthetic trappings, more than a just willingness to go against the norms and live a creative life. Just as silver is more than looking to the future. Copper is pursuing what is true to you. Your *Ástfríður* caregiver, they are copper, are they not? They followed their heart to a non-*Ástfríður* partner, and they are creative in a subtler fashion than we were in our last life. An injury does not bar you from choosing copper again. There is no wrong way to live as copper. None of the ways that the accident has changed you will deny you the ability to select copper for yourself. If you want it, that is."

"I'm sorry, this is just a lot."

"You are not the first *Ástfríður* to have an injury of this kind or this magnitude. You can make it a *part* of your identity, but it cannot be your *whole* identity. You can also choose not to have it define you at all. It's your choice. But you must make it before you can even hope to choose an *ahnhörn*. You can use whatever criteria you want to choose an *ahnhörn*, but you must be sure of what you want to claim as an identity first and how that identity fits the criteria for a metal."

Britt looked back down at the pebble on the ground. "The healers and my caregivers thought that the injury would fade, that it might be slow, but that eventually I would be better. I have good days where the headache is background noise and bad days where I can't get out of bed. I haven't really dealt well with the fact that this is probably how I will live the rest of my life."

The elder cocked their head to the side, a grin on their face, their eyebrows raised. "You don't say."

Britt laughed. "I should probably work on that. I don't think I can incorporate my injury into my identity. Not right now. I hate it, and I don't want to hate a part of me."

"You don't have to. You can change your mind—multiple times—if you want to. Following what feels right is copper. I changed my mind dozens of times about where I wanted to live. I wandered from clan to clan, to every island in the hold of the *Ástfriður* and then to Fayn and beyond."

"The humans of Fayn are so lucky they don't have to go through this."

"No, they have their own system they call gender, it is different but has just as many varied choices. I tried it while I was there, but it wasn't for me."

"I want to pick copper again. But a part of me doesn't want to, and that part has nothing to do with my injury."

"There are many things that prevent any copper *ahnhörnu* from following their heart. And there are many ways to acknowledge the desire but also the impossibility, impracticability, or inability to follow that desire. Copper isn't about whims or flights of fancy, but an ongoing commitment to examine who you are in that moment and do your best to be true to that. I don't say this to be dismissive of the struggle you have, and will likely always have, with the symptoms of your injury."

"I can be copper and injured."

"Absolutely."

That tiny affirmation sent off a shockwave of small but significant shifts inside Britt. How much of their longing for copper was because they were afraid that if they sought it, it would be denied? How much was wrapped up in a sense of loss? But knowing that it could be theirs, if they wanted it freed them in a way to choose something else.

They looked up at their shadow. "I know what I want."

"Do you? Will you choose copper again?"

"No, not this time."

Their shade smiled, eyes like fireflies and that twinkle of mischief, and watched as Britt drew the metal from the ground, coaxing it out with song and sweat, magic and will. With all the care that one should have for the blood of the Gods, Britt shaped it, magic heating it between their hands, making it pliable and malleable. They spun the metal into thread and wove it into swirling patterns and latticework curves.

The time passed quickly. Britt's former self observed as they crafted a beautiful circlet, a base that rested on the forehead and rose to a glistening horn. The sun, which had barely crested the horizon when Britt had departed the Veil with the *Sång*, hung low in the western sky, its last rays kissing the earth goodnight.

"Silver, for the Seer, like your friend Arvid," the shade said, inspecting every detail as Britt set it down in front of them. "A more passive metal, but incredibly important."

"It's not done yet," Britt scolded. They removed their bracelet. It glowed between their hands, the red of the sunset on a clear day. They stretched the metal, spinning it thin, and then wrapped it around the silver horn. It was an uneven swirl, the silver clearly more prominent. But the copper accented it, entwining divination with will.

The metal cooled quickly, and Britt smiled at their past self while lifting the circlet and horn up. They held it over their head, an almost imperceptible pause, eyes locked with the Britt-that-was. They closed their eyes and their hands released the circlet, allowing it to fall onto their head. It felt right against their skin, and they spent a moment absorbing the new ways it allowed them to communicate with the veins of the Gods.

Britt wasn't expecting the shade to stick around, having fulfilled their purpose—not even to say goodbye. So when they opened their eyes and found themselves alone again in the woods, they were not disappointed.

SILVER

A CAREGIVER IS NOT normally allowed to go with their charge for their *väljahnhörn;* they are to stay behind, to make food, and to prepare for the feast after the choosing. But Ylve was not normal. I was not normal. Ylve kept me safe; loved me when no one else could. A *tonå* who still cannot summon metal, a *tvära* with no history in any of the records of our people: me. Astrid, the one who is ugly, unlovable, and useless. Ylve kept me safe from those who might realize my defect. Ylve—who ensures that no one could get close enough to notice—went with me.

Ylve accompanied me silently, secretly. The path from the village to the Lake of the Mirror is not difficult, and not far. Leaving first the outermost of the thatch-roofed houses, past the fields of crops and grains, pastures for our goats and cows, and finally into the warm woods. How Ylve secreted themself away as the *Sång* held my hand through the fields of lavender, I did not know. Maybe Ylve was already in the forest while the *Sång* was still praying with me in our temple.

The *Sång* led me to the Lake, watched me wade into it, and told me I would know what to do from there. Every *Ástfríður* knows that they return from *väl-jahnhörn* no longer a *tonå;* they return transformed into an *ahnhörnu*. One who has their *ahnhörn*. One who wears the metal circlet proudly on their brow, one who has chosen their metal, or been chosen by it, and forged it and bent it to the shape they want their life to take.

One who has called to the metal deep in the earth's roots and bent it to their desires. Every *Ástfriður* knows this.

But there is more to it, some step between wading into the waters of our Lake—the waters of the Lake of the Mirror, the sacred place of our clan—and walking back into our village. No one talks of that in-between. No one discloses what happens. I assumed that maybe it was an individual thing, everyone finding their own ways, their own meanings and rituals, maybe it was a feeling. Maybe it was something deep in the *Ástfriður* blood that tells us what to do, that there was some secret that was unlocked, released once the waters touch skin. Or maybe there were instructions, given by the *Sång*. Some ritual that is taught or shown while praying at the temple. Or demonstrated once they were at the Lake. But as the *Sång* walked away into the mist and back into the lush forest that circled the Lake, I realized I was lost.

I realized young that I was not a normal *Ástfriður*. I could not hear the song of the metal in the ground, I could not follow its melody. If I could not do that, I could not create an ahnhörn. That was why Ylve was with me that day. But even they would not tell me what came in between, this spiritual aspect. If my blood could not harmonize with metal, then it could not accompany whatever aetherial aspect there was to this ceremony.

I had sat with Ylve at the edge of the lake, surrounded by the towering trees and lush vegetation. On a clear night one could sit at the edge and see the stars sparkle above, and their reflections ripple below. They chose obsidian for me, dark and deep and dangerous. That was what I was, something that threatened not just our clan, Lake of the Mirror, but all *Ástfriður*. An anomaly. My existence was counter to the ways of the *Ástfriður*.

We kept ourselves blocked off from the rest of the world, from those who would steal our metals, destroy our forests, and sully our lakes. A single port allowed us to trade with the outside world, though the people of Fayn and other nations have asked for more, and pirates have tried to sneak upon the shores of the Veil: the guarded archipelago of the *Ástfriður*. And I was unable to call metal, just as those of the outside world. I could be taken for an intruder, a fake, a spy, a thief.

I was a danger. I could be one of those acolytes of the new gods of the outside world, here to evangelize, to covertly attempt to convert. I could be a member of one of the old factions of the ancient sorcerers, trying to gain an upper hand in their centuries-long wars, trying to steal our magic for their pointless conflict. The strife of the world outside the Veil was not one we wanted to intrude on our peace.

And only my caregiver loved me enough to lie for me, anyone else who knew this might ostracize me, banish me, or worse. As it was not many came near me; my features too odd, cheeks too sharp, nose too long. Hair too coarse, eyes the disturbing shade of night. No one came near me for these reasons; and then I gave them reason to beyond that. I was just as graceful, just as light of foot, just as merry on celebration days and somber on days of sorrow. But I did not speak, I did not converse, I did not interact with those of Lake of the Mirror unless necessary. Only Ylve loved me, despite all of this. I did not need anyone else.

The day they sat with me, forged the ahnhörn —that circlet with the spiral horn on top that attuned us more with the metal— and put it around my head was one of the last days I could plausibly conceal my defects. A *tonå* was not expected to perform their metal magics, not expected to prove themselves an adept wielder. But now I would be. I would be expected to bend the metal at celebrations, to create beautiful artwork with it. How could I possibly hide it now?

Ylve slipped away as silently as they had arrived once they handed that circlet to me. Their red hair at twilight, a bonfire in the night, smile alight with pride, though I did not know for what.

I made my way home, passing the wooden cottages, the brick houses, the stone paths that wound their way through the homes, through the wisteria, the lilac trees and the rose bushes. Ylve's friends were waiting, the small dining room table was not large enough to accommodate all. It was more a celebration for Ylve than myself, I took to my bed early. Within the next few weeks, I would have my own cottage, a new bed, a new table... but how many friends to fill it with?

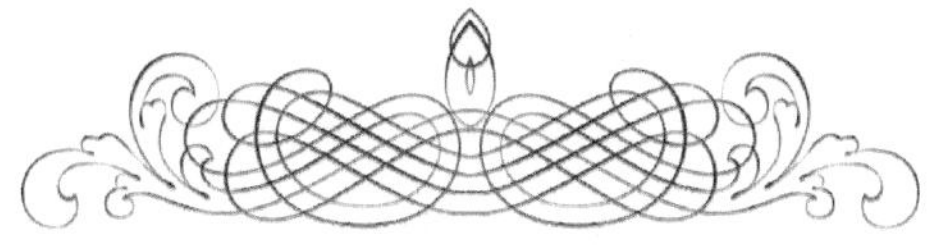

I learned to dance, to distract. A graceful spectacle that would make people question no further, to keep them from seeing what inwardly I was missing. To sway so succinctly with song, my every step sonorous and surreal, that they forgot that there even was an inner me to concern themselves with. Dance so beautifully that metal was not needed to convey what was felt, no need to spin silver to tell the world who I was.

I joined with the acolytes of the temple, who's devotions were done through art created without metal, expressing the loyalty of the whole self to our way of life, to our forests and lakes and mountains and shores.

We were more than the metal we could wield, more than the gift the Veil gave us. Practicing my twirls at the temple, and my leaps the lake, *pas de chat* about my cottage, spinning as I made my way down the streets. I gave off a sort of pride, and happiness as I went about my daily business. I was looked upon as an elegant gift to the community, but not an individual. I wanted more, wanted to be seen for who I was, not just the art I could create. I realized quickly that it was better this way, safer.

My grace and elegance quickly earned me the lead position of the temple dancers. The fellow acolytes were not my friends, however, though it should have felt the safest to solicit their friendship.

At festivals, my dancing was my contribution, eyes trained on my outward movements, and not my inner failings. Though I was appreciated by everyone for my arts, I was careful to maintain the distance that had

at first been foisted upon me, and that I now embraced.

A DRIAN ARRIVED A YEAR later. At first, they seemed so vibrant, so alive. Inge sought them out immediately, and they sought Inge's company in turn. Adrian laughed and sang and flirted and filled the room with their silver light just as much as Inge did with their gold. Adrian's soft white hair swept behind them, always seeming to be caught in the wind, a sheet of silken silver.

But I found myself gravitating toward them, too. And I was surprised when they returned my affections. It was intoxicating. They alone could dance as well as I, with as much grace and the sentiment to match it.

It is not enough to dance, to know the steps and the choreography. We both found excuses to practice dancing together; beautiful, bashful excuses.

Adrian had been *tvära* in the clan of the Tree of Morning. But they did not explain why they came here, what they sought. We found a record of them having been born into our clan long ago, though only that one time. But now they stayed with us. We asked why they came, and then we asked why they stayed. Their answer was always a shrug and a smile. They were tvära, many times over.

The questions they posed faded in my mind. Those mysteries did not matter to me, only that Adrian was here now. Only that I had a dance partner that I could find myself, one day, being more than honest with.

Ylve took an instant interest in Adrian, too. Ylve did not seem inclined to show the newcomer kindness as they had shown me, but still sort of protectiveness. A curiosity that seemed academic, removed and clinical. But still interested. Ylve kept close to Adrian as much as they could and ensured that they were given all the same respect that the rest of the clan gave to each other.

They quickly became as much a fixture in the clan as Inge and myself, though Inge was everywhere in the clan. Inge chose gold and silver, and their ahnhörn was thick, sturdy, and shone like the sun and the moon embraced. Everyone thought that Inge was destined to be the next *sång*. They, too, were different. In a way that attracted people, that moved them, that made a room bright and airy. They were not outcast; they were not on the fringes. They did not want to be. They did not need to be. But different from the rest of the clan, all the same.

Inge sometimes looked through me, as if they did not see me, which for some reason caused an ache in my heart I could not explain. I did not want to be perceived. Sometimes it felt like they were looking in me. Seeing that which I wanted to hide. They smiled at me, they tried to befriend me just as much as they wanted to with Adrian. Again, I longed to reach out to them. But they might see me; I feared that something would change if they did. Their attunement to the veins of the earth might expose me as a fraud. I kept Inge at a distance by wrapping myself in a dress of aloofness. Became what the village wanted to see. It was better this way.

It soon became apparent that the community thought it would make much more sense if Adrian were with Inge. While our synergy in dance was unparalleled, though we danced together as if we were extensions of the other's body, the village decided that we were ill-suited for each other otherwise. Our temperaments too unaligned.

As time went on the three of us became more and more a symbol of the clan; a part of the village that seemed inexplicably to define the village itself. But still separate, still not fully able to be ourselves. None of us were individuals, though Inge and Adrian were cherished in ways that I was not. Everyone thought that they knew who Inge and Adrian were as individuals; projected upon them all their beliefs about who those two should be; gave them the traits that they thought best described the characteristics valued in our village. All of this done while I was someone that they could not ever approach, I had been deemed too distant. They were living breathing embodiments of the Lake of the

Mirror. I was their static but beautiful shadow; an entity that could not be touched, only admired from afar. The village wanted to touch Inge and Adrian, to imagine themselves to be close to them. They deemed me to be untouchable. A beauty that was cold, feared because it might shatter if you tried to touch it. Best to leave it alone.

The three of us were always asked to perform. Adrian's voice, and my dance meshed so musically with Inge's metal arts. We would all dance together, since, and weave our bodies in and out of the gold and bronze and copper that Inge would call upon, the silver that Adrian summoned. For just one second, for just those minutes, I wanted to reach out to Inge. To truly make our performance one where we were truly all in sync. We all put everything we had into those performances, filled our movements and our bodies and our voices with all of the emotion that we could, all of our individual passion. But still.

I left these events feeling hollow, and an uneasy sense that I was missing something. Maybe I had left my shawl behind or had forgotten to return something I had borrowed. The feeling persisted until I decided to put it out of mind, and only the touch of Adrian's hands on my shoulders, or his fingers through my hair could alleviate it. Though, never entirely.

THOUGH SLOW IN A way that no one else seemed to notice, Adrian's eyes grew different, but not as mine were. Almost empty, hollow of all expression of emotion. They became too light, too round. Slowly, they withdraw. The silver of their ahnhörn dulled and filled with nicks. It looked as though it would break at any moment. Delicate, fragile.

Though they ate, they seemed to constantly be malnourished, though they sang, they seemed to constantly be flat, beauty no longer backed by feeling. Though Adrian had a rich and clear voice, they rarely spoke now. Soon they gained just as much of a reputation as I had. Not the same sort, but still Adrian became unapproachable. People spoke of this as if it were my doing, they still admired and envied the beauty that Adrian brought, but were off put by the changes in Adrian's personality. I could not believe that no one else saw these physical changes, no one else noticed the ways in which Adrian's body had changed, how the change in their behavior was correlated to the change in their physicality.

They pulled away from me, not entirely, though perceptibly. But I clung on, held out hope that this was temporary. That Adrian was just sick, that it had nothing to do with me. There was some illness wrecking their body, and it was not some part of my wrongness infecting them. The physical deterioration they were experiencing was not a result of their closeness to my broken body.

But as they grew weaker, Inge approached them more and more, Inge smiling at them. Inge casting their bright glow upon Adrian's shaded face.

"They should be yours, Astrid," Ylve said. I turned to face them, not knowing how they had silently slipped behind me. I set my book down on the table beside me. "Hmm?"

"Adrian."

"What do you mean?" The wind sang quietly; I stood and walked to the edge of the patio, resting my hands on the railing. It was too perfect of a spring day to stay indoors.

"*Isjälsfrä*." They joined me, resting on their elbows as they looked out into the fields my home bordered.

"Nonsense. I would know if they were."

"You surely have felt it, though. You may not have recognized it for what it is, though." They turned around, their back against the railing, and looked at me, appraising me.

I thought back to all the times I had spent with Adrian. And then the ways Ylve would assess them from the background. The ways my stomach seemed to drop when I saw Adrian and Inge laugh together or share meals together now. But *Isjälsfrä* were rare, our rebirth cycle meant there might be hundreds of years between when we left and when we returned. A person you were meant to be with, through all your lives, even if separated by decades and clans... it was only a theory from the ancients. From before we scattered across the Veil. Before we became Lake of the Mirror, Mountain at Dawn, Valley of the Gray Mist, and other clans in which one might be alive while the other was still floating, waiting for their next birth.

But Ylve thought Adrian and I were *Isjälsfrä*. The Elder, the historian, a council member, could not be wrong. They knew me as much as another could.

They are the only one who could love you who isn't me, not spoken by Ylve, but there. The air weighed down with that statement as Ylve stared at me.

T HE LAKE IS WHERE *Sång* have always gone to find a new *spädba*. They have a dream that a soul has come back to live a life again, and the next morning they go to the Lake. A basket of leaves, shells, and metal appears and floats from the center of the lake to the shore, inside: a sleeping *spädba*. The Sång collects the newly returned, cradles the little one in their arms, and walks back to the village. A caregiver is assigned, and so the journey begins anew for an *Ástfriður* soul. Ylve would tell me of how tiny I was when I was brought back, a trait I still carried as the shortest in our village, and how well-behaved I was even as I grew.

When Adrian and I sat at the shores of this Lake, my head resting in their lap, I wanted to ask them stories of their own youth. At first, they had been profusive with their tales. Trouble they had gotten into, their own stories of the Tree of Morning, and how the *Sång* found *spädba* cradled in their Tree's branches.

But now, having taken sick with some unexplainable illness, they only spoke short sentences as they ran their hands through my hair. The dulling of their silver taking a toll even on their disposition. But still, they did not shy away from looking into my shadowed eyes, they did not question me when they would summon silver from the earth on our dates and I did not call my own metals. They did not comment on my strange features, or look at me differently despite them.

I could speak to them of feelings I had never shared. I wanted to believe Ylve. It seemed so natural now: that I should love Adrian. I held their hand and tried to imagine I could feel the iron in their blood, calling back to mine: the first time I thought maybe I was not so broken as I thought I was. Maybe I had been so empty before that I could not even recognize what I was missing, that it had been there the whole time, and now Adrian had made me alive, and slowly I would learn how to be *Ástfriður*. That I had not, in fact, been living a lie, but just living as a shade. There was a current between us, I could feel it. I could feel the flow of something between us. I could not possibly be imagining it.

Since my conversation with Ylve, I had shut out the idea that I was the reason for the waning of their light.

I could be enough for them.

INGE ASCENDED TO THE council, and with their acceptance of the position they took on the role of Scryer. They continued to be beautiful, continued to speak to everyone with a genuine kindness that left me confused. But I chaffed now when I saw them speak with Adrian, which they continued to do with even greater a frequency, with even more fervency. I could not quite place why I felt my stomach drop when I saw the two together. I did not want to see Inge with them, but it was not that there was someone with Adrian, but that Inge was conversing with someone with any degree of true familiarity; a mask set aside.

Inge would lock themself in the temple and watch the liquid mirror in all their divine finery, waiting and watching. A shifting surface made of fluid metal mixed with the waters of the Lake drawn under a full moon. If they saw anything in it, I never could know. The quick glances I made toward our sacred object when I left the temple after a dance devotional showed me nothing.

But Inge would sigh, and then leave. I watched them through the doors to the dance rooms. Sometimes they smiled to themself, sometimes they would wring their hands, and others yet they would come out looking expressionless. It was the latter that disturbed me the most. It was the latter that seemed so unsettling. Our shining sun, our lively light, suddenly shaded. They looked like a ghost. In all situations, they seemed to caught up in another world to notice that I was there, watching.

They were leaving the temple one day, that far-away look in their eyes, and they tripped. I did not think, just sprang toward them. Grabbed them before they fell to the ground and righted them. I almost dropped them, though, when I felt a spark where my hand touched their skin. They smoothed their robes, righted their ahnhörn, and looked at me. The sort of look that went beyond seeing, beyond searching. They had looked in me before, but this was something deeper, something more intense.

My hand reached for the copper necklace that hung around my neck, a gift from Ylve. The metal was cold, though. Colder than it normally was. I had never known the warmth of metal that others spoke of. Yet the necklace was still a comfort, but it held no protection—no reassurance, no safety —right now. I was undone in their eyes, and I knew instantly that they saw all of me. And all of my deficiencies.

Their eyes widened, and then they ran from me.

I WAITED, MY HEART racing in my chest for hours. I did not know that one could be both exhausted and unable to sleep. I did not know that one could be starving without the desire to eat. That one could feel time dilating into eternity and compressing into minutes. That one could search for anything to do and then do nothing at all.

I waited days, but Inge never shared my secret. I waited weeks, yet they never knocked on my door to speak with me. Whatever it was that they had seen had frightened them. And yet. No one approached me, no one came to me to cast me out, no one arrived to exile me, to call me a traitor and bury me in the earth. No one came to inflict upon me any of the terrors that had crept into my mind on those long and lonely nights. No one came to demand that I confess to my most hidden secrets, the ones so terrifying I did not want to admit them even to myself.

Instead, everything continued as normal. Ylve did not say anything, did not suspect. Surely, they would tell me if they thought someone knew how broken I was. Surely, they would warn me, or even protect me, if Inge had told anyone on the council, if Inge had disseminated even a hint that they knew something was broken inside of me.

My fears and anxieties must have been apparent to Adrian, though. For who else would truly understand? Adrian came to see me every day, every day we would go to the Lake and I would lay on the grass. I would swim and they would give the smallest smile. It was small, but it was mine. It was only for me. I was the only one they shared this bit of their soul, their silver was the moon, and my obsidian the night. This Lake was our reflection. I felt as though I could walk across it, not a ripple following behind. Floating above it. Sometimes I imagined I could dance until the trees joined me. Sometimes I imagined that when they would sing along the wind would respond in glorious harmony, the wind's whistle matching their voice. Together we would fill the night with magic.

"Do you love me?" I asked them every day.

They nodded. Of course, they did, I should have known. I should not even have had to ask. We were *Isjälsfrä*. The words should not need to be spoken. But I asked them every day, and every day they affirmed that they did. Every day my stomach churned as they would stand and hold out their hand. Every day I would take it and follow them back to the village, back to real life.

I would look at them as we returned, the night still ever-present, and all our clan in bed, look in their eyes, and see my own reflection. Though their eyes had clouded since the disease had started to take its toll, I could still see who they truly were. And they saw who I was. I was enough for them, even if Inge told everyone everything, still I was sure I would be enough for them. I had to be enough for them. I hoped I was enough for them.

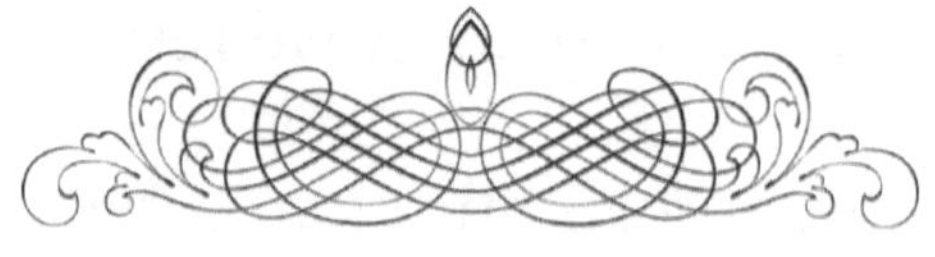

"**D**O YOU LOVE ME?"

"Yes, I love you."

"Do you love me?"

"Yes, I love you."

"Do you love me?"

"Yes, I love you."

Can you ask a ghost to love you? For that was what they were becoming. More and more each day, they faded. They shed their substance as one would shed a shawl. Can you ask a body of mist, hollow and cold, if they love you? It must be real; it has to be real. Do not think about it. Do not think about it. Adrian loves me.

They have to... they have to.

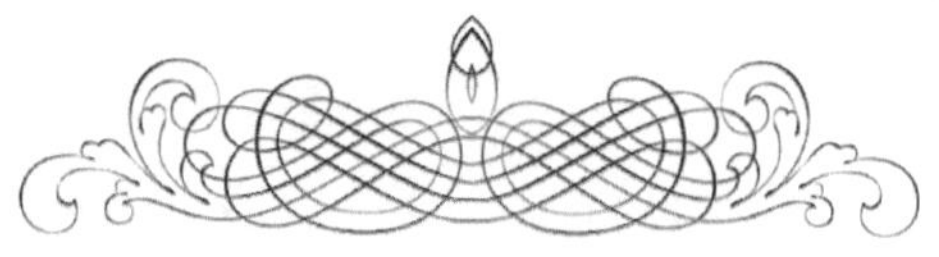

"ASTRID," CAME A VOICE from outside of my door. I peeked around the window in my dining room, but I recognized that voice anyway. The bright song that could only belong to one person: Inge. They must surely be here to bring me before the council, to shame me and banish me. I put on a dark shawl and walked to the door, opening it slowly, as if I could stall my doom, still yet conceal myself.

"Hello, Inge." I did not know what else to say.

"May I come in?" they asked, haltingly.

I opened the door wide to let them in, waved to a couch. They wrung their hands and looked around, seeming to take in everything in my home and nothing at all. They sat down, leaning forward in the chair. I tried to settle into the armchair across from them, but the cushions were now as cold and hard as stone.

"Why...are you here?" I asked.

I did not expect what she said next. "Ylve wants to be sång." It came out as if it were one word, and then buried their head in their hands. After a pause, they looked up at me, guilt in their eyes. I could not tell what for.

I blinked, and they continued to stare, searching my face for something. But then my stomach fell: I had not known this; I was owed nothing by my caregiver after I became ahnhörnu, but I expected that this might be something they would share. I had moved out, I had settled myself in my own home, I no longer relied on Ylve. I became family of the clan, the whole of the Lake of the Mirror. Ylve was no longer tied to me nor I to them. And yet. They did not tell me of this ambition. How long had they harbored it? Why did they? I could understand not telling me when I was a tonå, but now? All those years later I was surely owed this knowledge.

The only one who might love you as I do.

They told Inge.

No one else would love you.

They told Inge.

Hide away, no one could love you if they knew.

They told Inge.

"Astrid? Astrid?" Inge said. They said it as if they knew me. As if I was a friend they cared for.

"I do not know why you are here." I softened my voice as much as I could, tried to make it melodic, but formal. I did not want them to see me either break down in despair or explode with rage. They had told Inge.

"I know that many think that I will be called to be the next sång."

"I do not see how this should be important to me." I sat back in my chair; arms crossed. "Whoever is called is called. It is the Lake that chooses. It is not something that we can choose or influence."

"I do not think it is either of us." They looked down, staring at their hands as they fidgeted with the hems of their long sleeves. "The mirror showed me—"

I stood up; my fists clenched and then unclenched. I took a breath. "I do not care what your mirror showed you. I do not care who the Lake chooses. I do not care about the council or elders or any of that. This is not my concern; this is not something I am involved in."

"But I saw you, too. And Adrian..."

I sat back down, I could feel myself grow cold, growing numb. "This is about my magic."

"Well, yes. And no."

No one else will love you.

"Get out," I said, barely a whisper. If I didn't whisper, I would shout. "Just please get out."

No one else...

The tears were about to pour out, and I could not let anyone, let alone Inge, see me cry.

"But Adrian—"

No one else... no one at all. Never good enough for anyone.

"Please. Just please go."

"Astrid, please. Let me explain." Again, they said my name as one might say the name of a loved one. And my traitorous mind wanted to return that affection, that connection, the closeness that that tone implied. Inge stood up and reached their hand out to me. I shook my head. They drew it back and fidgeted with their robe before silently leaving, I did not even hear the door latch.

No one else.

But there had been no one all along.

INGE APPROACHED ADRIAN THE next day asking them to join them for breakfast. Inge invited Adrian over for dinner. Inge searched them out for weekly rituals. It was as though they slowly melded into one being. One entity instead of their separate selves. I dared not approach Adrian while Inge was with them. But then Adrian stopped asking me to the Lake. Our daily meetings becoming less and less frequent.

I was not enough; they had forsaken me. Inge did not want me around them. I could not puzzle out how exactly it all fit together. But I was not someone who could be around Adrian. And a council member knew so, a potential *sång* had seen something in that mirror that warned of something. Something that meant I could not be with Adrian.

How could that be? We were *Isjälsfrä*. We were *Isjälsfrä*....

I had not loved Adrian enough yet, I was far from loving them enough still.

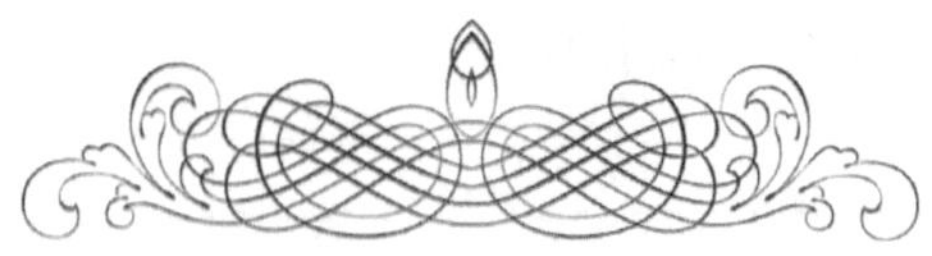

I WANTED TO APPROACH Ylve again and ask them what was going on but could not bring myself to do so. My hand would raise to touch my necklace from them, but then I remembered I had taken it off. They would try to talk to me as they always had, cheerful and bright. The smile always there. But I could never tell if they noticed the change inside of me. I would curl in on myself, and I felt as though I could not breathe. I would steer the conversation to trivial topics, away from anything that might cause my eyes to well with tears. The only times we broached a subject bordering on importance was when they would tell me that I had to fight for Adrian. How I could not let someone else steal them away from me. How Adrian was the only one who could love me, that was not them.

In those moments I would square my shoulders, and as they spoke, I would consider ways to win Adrian back from Inge, beautiful perfect Inge. Who thought they were better than me, better for Adrian. I had to be more, love them more... But then I would deflate and steer the conversation again away from my caregiver's ever-insistent prodding for me to replace Inge in Adrian's affections. I did not want to talk to them about Adrian; if Ylve would not share their dreams with me, I could not share mine.

I listened to the murmurs and whispers in the village, wondering if others knew of my caregiver's desires, if it was public knowledge now or secreted inside the council only. One would think that even if it were confidential to the council, still they would trust me enough to tell me. But they did not.

T HOUGH I DARE NOT even speak the words in my mind, dare not acknowledge the wordless feeling that would flitter through my mind, I sometimes wished that Inge would visit me again. That they would say my name with affection, that they would look at me as a loved one would.

No one else could love you... No one else would love you if they knew.

I dare not acknowledge that I hope that the spark I had felt the day that Inge tripped was not a prelude to disaster, but a prologue the dearest of relationships.

I could not feel these things, I could not acknowledge these desires.

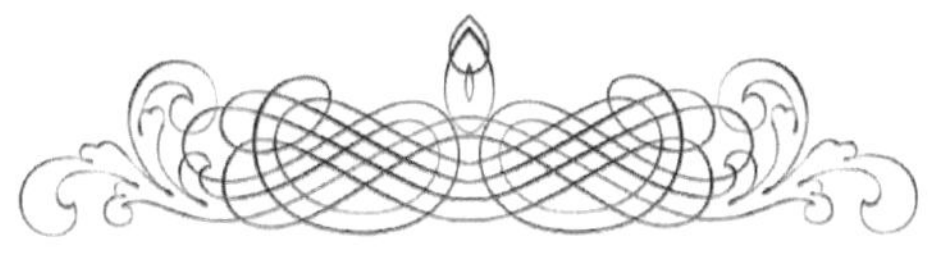

I STOPPED TRYING TO meet with Adrian. There was a mist around them now, as though they were lost in the fog of a cold night. Their features seemed to phase in and out of space, in and out of time. A ghost; more so than they had ever been. Though no one else seemed to see it. My stomach knotted, my chest tightened any time I saw them, flickering in and out of reality. I could feel a prickle, shivers down my spine. The air would grow cold around them. Yet no one said anything. No one approached them with concern.

Inge was everywhere. There was no escape. They were dancing; they were talking, they were visiting people, they were at the market trading wares, they were at the temple giving devotions. Where Adrian had grown cold, they had grown warmer; their head tipped to the sky, their face glowing. Sometimes I would cross their path, and they would look at me, head tilting toward their shoulder, hands momentarily falling to their sides. We would stand there, staring at each other while time stopped, arrested in a snow globe. Sometimes I thought I saw them open their mouth as if to speak, and their hand reaching forward before quickly falling again to their sides.

But then they would slowly turn away, lifting their head again to smile at someone. My stomach would sink, my lips pressed together as I, too, turned away, looking at the ground. Sometimes I wanted them to say whatever it was they wanted to say, to approach me, and... Sometimes I wished I could break whatever glass trapped us in the stillness of the temporary

un-space. Sometimes I wanted to reach my hand out,

too.

I WENT TO THE Lake; though it was a late summer night, the air was filled with the weight of winter's promise. The wool shawl I wore could not even be called armor against the chill; it breached the silk of my skin and invaded my bones, conquered my blood, overthrew my heart. My breath became indistinguishable from the fog. I paid it no mind. I abdicated, I surrendered. I accepted. The cold made it easier for my body to quickly join my mind in the oblivion of dissociation. Frigid rejection. Rejection from others, my own bitter denial of myself. These memories I saw so clearly, but so desperately wanted to shatter as ice.

I did not want those feelings that had kindled inside of me. I wanted to feel anything except the thoughts that blazed in my soul, burnt my heart. These emotions might be seared into my being; better to feel nothing. I did not have to worry about anyone else; at the Lake, there was no judgement, no doubts. No emptiness. It did not matter if I caught sick. It did not matter, there was no one to worry over it.

Harmony rippled in the wind as water and stars sang together, lapping at the shore. The chirps of those nocturnal creatures awakening joined to take their own chords for this sonata. Breathing easy, in tune, I dipped my feet into the water. No pains or aches in my stomach, no tightness in my throat.

The Lake greeted me as though I were a child coming home, embracing me as a parent would a wayward child. *We have missed you*, the stars said. *We did not know where you went*, the water wept.

"I am home now," I said, not knowing to whom or to what I was speaking. It felt right to say it, though. Words fleeing my mouth before I could fathom what I was hearing, consider their meaning, or realize that I was conversing back.

I floated, and floated, and floated. Though the silver of Adrian was missing, I still felt as though I were part of the stars, part of the night sky. Part of this, whatever this was. It was different than when Adrian was here, somehow it was more intense; it sunk under my skin and burrowed into my bones, it cast out the cold that had conquered them. The cold that I had wanted, accepted: gone. But the water and the stars still kept at bay the bonfire I had been trying to escape.

I held my hands up as if I could catch a star. For the slightest moment, I thought the stars responded, a soft shiver down my arm, the caress of a loved one.

Don't leave us again, the water whispered.

Why did you abandon us? the stars sobbed.

A whirlwind, a tempest of commotion and chatter witnessed through a gauzy shroud, specters rushing past me. I had no form to try to tear away the viscous veil that separated me from them. The fabric pressed against me, immobilized me while these ghosts drew near, suffocating me.

Stay, stay, stay.

My breath was stolen from me. The air whispered images in my ears, planted sounds in my skin as it escaped. It pushed my past waking and into dreaming, or maybe I leapt into that emptiness, willing to follow the shadows to rivers that promised to school in the art of shedding memories.

Sister who was stolen across the seas.

Hidden in the shrouded trees.

Sister, sister. Finally found.

Walking on the evil ground.

Sister, sister. Where have you been?

Sister, sister. Join us again.

Starlight cut through the sheer curtain, bringing me back from the brink of oblivion. The voices echoed: surrounding me, encompassing me. Sweeping through me. It was more than song, more than beauty, more than hope or peace or elation. It was more than color, more than just the night. I was the stars; I was their reflection on water. I was the night sky.

The stars loved me; saved me from whatever was haunting me. I was good enough for them, good enough for the night sky, the deep and the darkness. That stretch of time where people feared that there was possibly danger in the shadows. Dark, deep, danger.

Though I returned every night, I never paused to consider that one word. Sister. It was a word from outside the safety of the *Ástfriður* woods. But it did not matter, that word. I could not fathom its meaning, but they said it with such a familiarity that I knew they meant it as an endearment. I belonged to the stars, I belonged with the stars. Even if it was just a feeling in my mind, I finally felt as though I had some sort of magic. Though, like the word sister, I did not want to consider that it came from anywhere but the Veil.

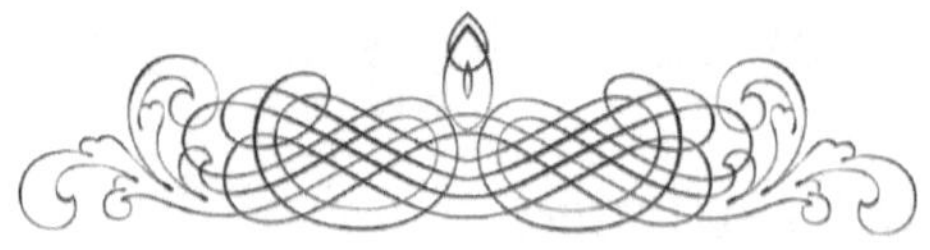

T HE *SÅNG* GREW WEAKER and spoke often of their return to the Lake. When Inge had told me, all those months ago, that Ylve sought to be the next sång, I thought they were speaking of some far-off time, years, decades, centuries. It was a shock, no one seemed to understand. The *Sång* was so strong, so young still. But within the span of months, we watched them fade. They took on the same coldness that followed Adrian, the same flicker that made them seem out of time. A stutter, as if they were moving slower–or perhaps, quicker–through time than the rest of us. People noticed their weakness, their frailty, but not the alien mist that seemed to circle them, to pull them temporarily out of our plane. Just as no one had noticed when Adrian entered this strange world that only occasionally crossed with ours.

I knocked on Inge's door.

It opened slowly, just a crack as she peaked out to greet me. Their brow furrowed. "Astrid…"

"May I," I swallowed. "May I come in?"

For a moment I thought they would quietly send me away, citing some excuse to save both of us our pride.

"Of course," they finally said. "Take a seat. Do you want some tea? I was brewing it fresh just now. I wasn't expecting anyone today, but I always have peppermint tea in the afternoon. My caregivers always did, too. I suppose that's where I learned the habit. The tea always—" They stopped abruptly. "I'm sorry. I should ask you why you are visiting. Not that I mind that you are visiting, I just wasn't expecting it, seeing as you... Oh, I mean..." They looked around their living room, suddenly extremely interested in the details of their own home.

"I have some questions, about Adrian. And about the *Sång*. I know I said it is none of my business, and I know you have been trying to keep me from Adrian. I do not know why, I know I am too different... Well, you know... but maybe you thought I was... not the best influence." I was as diplomatic as they had been. I swallowed. They looked to the side, their arms wrapping around them.

"I..."

"I understand why you think I may be a danger," I spat out, cutting them off. "But I do not know why you have not told anyone what you saw, that day... and I have not done anything—"

"You aren't a danger to anyone," they said, turning quickly to face me. "Not at all, not even a little bit. You wound me that you would think I harbor such feelings toward you. You insult me by thinking I would try to have you cast out. Is that what you have been thinking this whole time? I didn't try to take Adrian from you. You withdrew from them. I love them, yes. Have fallen in love with them while you were hiding in the night, but I am not so..."

"You do not think I am a danger?"

"No. No! Why would I!?"

"Because you saw..." I scrunched my face. Not wanting to say the words that felt most appropriate. Empty. Hollow. Nothing. "Something that made me... that day when you..." I shook my head. "Something is wrong with Adrian. That is why I am here, and something is wrong with the *Sång*." I slumped into the chair, looking down at my hands balled up in my lap. "They seem lost? Away?"

"You feel it, too." Not a question from them.

"I can see it," I said.

Inge paced. The golden child of our Lake of the Mirror. The *Ástfríður* who laughed, who sparkled, who brought joy to every room. They were nervous. I thought back to all of those times before that I had seen them be anything but a shining sun. All the times they let their mask drop. We were both different than the rest of the clan, and they had their own way of maintaining the persona that the clan needed them to wear.

"What do you mean when you say 'see' it?"

"They flicker in and out, they disappear into the air and appear a second later. They move as if they are walking through water, their form rippled. Their bodies, Adrian's and the *Sång's*, are out of phase."

"You can see this?"

"Surely as I can see you solidly before me."

"It isn't a feeling? This isn't some pretty metaphor for something you can sense?"

"No, Inge, no! There is something wrong, and I came here because you had spoken of this before. Why? And why to me? You just said I was not a danger. Then what do you think I have to do with this? Adrian is... I cannot lose them." I cannot lose the only person who may ever be able to love me. The only person for whom I have a hope of ever being enough. And I cannot lose them to you...

"Because you are different."

"That is a way of saying it, yes."

"The Mirror shows me many horrible things," they said. They hung their head, as if it were weighed down. Their shoulders slumped. "It is a gift; it is a curse.

I didn't ask for it! I didn't ask for it..." They looked off into the distance, and I could not interrupt. Did not want to see whatever it was that they were seeing. "Excuse me, I am sorry." They shook their head.

"Go on. You were saying?" My throat constricted; I could barely breathe.

They tried to take a deep breath, and then another. But when they finally spoke, their voice cracked. "The *Sång* is dying. Adrian is dying!"

"Dying? That is impossible. *Ástfríður* do not die, we cannot die."

"But they are. They are! They are being stolen from the Veil, from the Lake of the Mirror, from this world. They won't come back, they won't re-enter the cycle, they will fade, and then..." They collapsed to the floor; no attempt to stop this flood of feeling. "I've been trying to stop it, I've been trying to stop it, I've been trying so, so hard. Astrid, believe me, I've been trying."

The sun of Lake of the Mirror. The Scryer of silver and gold. The *Ástfriður* who felt each pulse of metal beneath their feet, who could draw out copper and bronze and weave them as ribbons and shape them into art. The *Ástfriður* who was so attuned to these metal veins that they could hear the conversations of others far away if they cared to. Surely, surely the next *sång*. No one could sing with our precious metals the way they could, no one could live in such harmony with the earth, drink so deeply of its blood.

"I can't stop it. Please, Astrid. Help me."

"This is what you were trying to ask me about."

"Yes. Yes!" They kept crying. "I don't know what else to do. I just know what the Mirror says, and it says you can save them."

"What? How! I am just a broken *Ástfríður*, one who cannot even sense metal let alone bend it!" I threw my *ahnhörn* to the ground. "It is a fake, it is a fake. Ylve made it for me to hide my brokenness! I am nothing. Whatever your Mirror says, it must be wrong. The *sång* cannot be dying. Adrian cannot be dying. It's impossible!"

Inge wiped away their tears and went very still. I could barely tell if they were breathing. Slowly they looked up at me. Then back at the obsidian circlet and horn before them. Softly, gently they said, "You aren't broken, though."

I grunted.

"You aren't though. Why would you say that?" They furrowed their brow.

"You saw me. You know how broken I am."

Inge stared at me, open-mouthed.

"Ylve has made sure no one knew how broken I was, if they knew they might try to cast me out, to banish me, to say I was some spy or intruder from Fayn, one of their..."

"But you aren't broken, what do you mean?"

"I have no metal! You saw it! You saw it, I cannot feel it, cannot touch it! I am broken! You saw it!"

"You don't have metal? What? No, you do have..."

I fled before they could finish their sentence. I did not want to hear pretty lies. Did not want false assurances that I was not broken. Did not want pity.

I RAN TO THE Lake. Inge called out after me, cried out as I dashed away. How could Inge say that? I was found at the Lake, the *Sång* brought me to the village. Gave me to Ylve, I was raised here. I was *Ástfríður*. But I could not call metal, could not feel it, could not...How could I be anything but broken? I only felt anything when I was with Adrian...or with Inge...or with the stars... What else could you call that?

I dove into the Lake. I was broken, not enough for the earth to want to claim. Not enough for the Veil to want to bless. Not enough, too broken for the metal to search me out, to sing to me. I was not just broken;

I was not wanted. I was not enough. Why would Inge say that? Why would Inge tell me that I was not broken when I clearly was? Whatever they saw in me, whatever their mirror told them, I was broken.

I surfaced, and my reflection in the water seemed to speak to me. My reflection showed what I had always wished to be otherwise. My eyes too dark. My cheeks too sharp. My nose too long. My hair too coarse, too short. The thin, soft short fur that graced the skin of *Ástfríður* was not there. I was broken, not just a lack of metal; the brokenness shown through to mar my features.

Sister. Sister. What troubles you so?

Sister, sister. You were happy just a day ago.

I am not just broken. I am worse than that. It was not just that I did not fit in, that I was not enough. It was that I did not even belong; I was a mistake. I swam back to the shore, and collapsed on the mossy shore, my knees sinking into the mud.

Sister, sister. What brought you back here?

I laced my hands through my hair and pulled.

Sister, sister! What is it that you fear?

The ground reverberated each time I bent over to scream.

Sister, sister...

"No! Leave me alone! Just leave me alone! I am not your 'sister'. I am nobody. I am nothing. I am broken and I am not enough! I will never be enough..."

Why did I keep coming here? To the Lake? To the Lake that had not blessed me, the Lake that did not want me. Why did I keep coming back here?

Sister, sister...

"A STRID! ASTRID!" PLEASE go away. I was cold, I was wet. I was sore. And someone was looking for me. "Astrid. We've been looking for you all day! I swear we've circled the Lake a dozen times. Where were you?"

"Here. Just here." I looked up. Ylve and some of the other elders looked down at me. I could not muster the energy to stand up. I could not muster the energy to even care. Their look of concern meant nothing to me. I did not even care to think about where I was, or why people were looking for me. The waves of the Lake rolled over my feet, and the mud was caked in my hair, my hands sore from beating the ground over and over. But I did not care at all.

"We've circled this way more than once today," one of the elder's said. I buried my face back into the moss, not wanting to get up at all.

"I just came here to be alone. So please leave me alone."

"Inge says they haven't seen you since last night."

"Last... night? That is not right. All day?" This startled me back to some sort of awareness.

"Dear child, you've been missing for over a day now. And where is your... ah, it does not matter right now. We found you."

Sister, sister.

"I do not know what you mean. I just left Inge's a few hours ago." I ran my hand across the grass.

Sister, sister. What do you need?

Ylve sighed. "You must be sick. Let me carry you home."

Their arms felt foreign, both solid but far away, as they curled under me and pulled me off of the ground. The Lake stirred loudly, and the stars pulsed. The trees rustled despite the lack of wind. Ylve looked around, their brows knitted. I had never seen them look unsettled before. But they were too far away for me to care.

Sister! Sister! Don't let them steal you again!

Sister! Sister! Beware of their greed!

Sister, sister. They are not your kin,

Sister, sister.

A wind roared suddenly, the howl of it like a mourner, full of despair.

"Where is Frej? Someone go ahead and tell them to have a sick bed ready!"

"Who stole me?" I asked the stars, almost drowned out by the wails of the angry wind.

Ylve held me as they had when I was younger. Close to their chest. Smoothing my hair when I had fallen in the dirt, rubbing my shoulders when I complained of the cold. So near, loving me the way no one else could. But I recognized none of this now, it seemed unfamiliar now.

"Astrid. I'm so glad we found you."

Sister, sister. We finally found you.

"We were so worried."

Sister, sister. We've been so worried.

"Why?"

"Why wouldn't I be? I love you, remember?"

The only one who could love me knowing I was broken.

"The wind," they continued. "It worries me, too."

Sister, sister! Don't go away.

Please come back. Please stay.

INGE CLASPED THEIR HANDS over mine. I was, in fact, sick. I did not know what excuse they made to the healers for why they found me without my *ahnhörn*, why, instead, it had been in Inge's possession. I did not want to ask, no one commented on it to me. I just knew that when I awoke, it was on a nightstand beside me, and the copper necklace from Ylve was back around my throat.

Inge visited for long hours while I was with the healers. They would bring me news of events in the village, things I had never bothered to pay attention to before. The silly stories of goats that had gotten loose and caused trouble in the market square. Or bring books that they had borrowed from a neighbor. There was one that I particularly like, one written by someone from Valley of Fog; it was about someone who has half fish, and felt torn between worlds. I found it sad, but loved it anyway. When I was sent back home to continue to recover, Inge spent entire days with me. Sometimes, they stayed the night.

Butterflies, flowers, the sweetness of the morning's bread. The coming summer, the smell of the lavender thrown into the hearth. These: our topics of conversations. Our hands would brush when they handed me tea; each time the spark I had felt that day when I had caught them. My heart would race when I saw them staring at me over the rim of their mug. Their face would grow rosy when I smiled at them. But today–their palms warm as they held mine–we needed to speak of other matters.

"Share with me, please. What happened."

I had been avoiding talking about it. They had been pretending they did not know that there was something I was avoiding. "I cannot."

"You have to, though."

"It is not that, it is that it is almost impossible to describe. There were voices. No, one voice but many at the same time. They came from the stars, the ones in the sky and the ones on the water and from the wind that connects them. They told me I had been lost, or maybe stolen. The way they spoke to me, of me, about me. As if I was part of them and not of here."

Inge chewed their bottom lip.

"I swear I was only there a few hours. I do not know how I could have missed an entire day."

They seemed out of phase. Flickering. Stuttering. Echoes. Ghosts. Distortions.

"I believe that it felt like that to you." Inge stood up. They brought their face to mine, searched my eyes, their *ahnhörn* a hair's breadth away from mine. I nodded. They rubbed their ahnhörn against mine. I let them do this, I wanted to flinch back from the intimacy at first when I realized what they wanted, but instead, I closed my eyes and tried to imagine what it must feel like for them.

"They called me sister," I said, interrupting the moment as my throat tightened.

They pulled back. I looked away. "That's a word that lohyue use, and a word that the qatu-calla use, a word for people outside of the Veil."

"I know. But the stars think I am their 'sister'. I know it has no place in the Veil. But that is what the stars called me."

"Will you show me?"

"Show you?"

"What happens at the Lake when the stars speak to you."

"I suppose…" I hesitated. If the stars called me sister, the implications: I did not want to know. I took my dishes to the sink. I did not want any more of my breakfast.

"It will help them. Adrian."

"Tonight."

YLVE CAME BY JUST after Inge left for the morning. They brought a basket of breads and berries and set them out on the table before us. Taking the seat across from me they asked, "Has Inge been helpful? They come by every day."

"They have been a great help." I could only pick at the berries, and only for Ylve's sake.

"Good, I'm glad to hear it. Have they been able to help you figure out what happened that night? How you got so lost?" Their voice was soft, the soothing tone they used when I had fallen or cut myself when I was young.

"No." They had helped me hide how broken I was; the only one who could love me despite that brokenness.

"I was hoping they would be able to."

"And Adrian? I have not seen them visiting you." Their brow knitted; I could only assume why they were asking.

"No, no, they have not." Ylve should have known that Adrian was also bound to their bed, that Inge had also been attending to them.

"Ah. I shall talk to them, and see if they can stop by. They are yours, after all." Ylve did not seem to care that Adrian was also ill at all.

I looked away, suddenly entirely interested in a bird outside.

"I'm sorry I have been too busy to visit before." They smoothed away a wisp of hair that had loosed itself from their braid and coughed when I said nothing. "I've been very busy with council business."

I continued to keep my silence.

"I should have told you this sooner, Astrid. I am going to join the *väljasång*. I am going to undertake the ceremony and hopefully become the next *sång*. I know I can fulfill those duties. I was going to tell you the night that you disappeared, and since then I've been so busy. And I didn't want to disturb you. I didn't want to burden you while you were recovering."

"Inge told me already."

"Ah. I wish they hadn't, I should have been the one to tell you. You aren't my charge anymore, Astrid. But I will never stop thinking of you as such. I will never stop loving you." They smiled at me, and I wanted to smile back, wanted to remember what it had felt to trust them. But all I could manage was a grimace.

"When is the *väljasång*? Surely the *Sång* is not so weak that it would be soon. Surely their *väljanda* is still far away. They have only been here for a few decades; it is unheard of for the Lake to call someone back so soon!"

"They know it is time for their *väljanda*. We all know when *väljanda* is near for us. It is not so scary to return to the spirit world to await your next rebirth. And they know that it is nearly their time to wade into the Lake and be taken back home. You will know your time, too, when it comes. You are still so young, Astrid," they sighed and leaned back.

"I suppose."

"The *väljasång* will be in two weeks. The new *sång* will be given the official *ahnhörn* by the old, and then the old *sång* will depart. Don't frown, it is part of the cycle. And I know I can strengthen our clan, make it healthier, happier. I can put us back on the right path.

I can help us return to the roots of our culture; with my knowledge of our history and the vision for the future, I know I can serve well. Restore us to who we truly are. And I was hoping I would be able to tell you this first. When I become *sång,* when I am given that *ahnhörn,* I will stop being Ylve. I will have no name; I will have no concerns but that for the greater good of the *Ástfríður* of the Lake of the Mirror. But I will always, always love you." They reached across the table, took my hands, and held them tightly. "Always."

No one else could love you.

"And what if you are not chosen? What if you cannot call and shape the metal with the precision and heart that the *väljasång* requires? What if someone else is chosen?"

They looked down, hands loosening. "That won't happen. Don't worry about that, my Astrid."

"How do you know?"

"The stars will make it so. The stars have already told me."

Sister, sister.

INGE WAS WAITING OUTSIDE as the sun was setting. I threw a shawl over my shoulders and took their hand. I do not know why I took their hand as if I were leading them; we both knew the way to the Lake. But it felt important that I do, their hand was fire against the chill of the night. Every step reverberated through the woods, and I feared that an elder would hear us, or that Ylve would somehow know that I was slipping away when I should be recovering.

I assumed that Inge was being heavily watched; their decision to join *väljasång* was not a surprise, and their upbeat nature and sweet disposition made them more likely to be chosen than the others. But their natural kindness could not account for how much time they had been spending with the clan's most aloof member. We were an odd pair. We were both beauties of the village, but Inge was soft and warm. I was cold and sharp.

Diamonds danced upon the shallow waves of the Lake, starlight collecting on the sapphire ripples as if they were night-blooming flowers. The water consuming the moon like nectar. The dark encompassed the reedy shore, casting a cobalt haze upon the scene, now punctuated only by the gold that Inge wore upon their brow.

But I looked deeper and saw a hazy shadow over the Lake that could not be explained by a fog or the magic between stars and water. The constellations could not account for the image that flickered in and out, there was something in the water that was more than shadow, more than shade. Out of phase. A song surrounded me. Though Inge showed no signs of hearing this symphony.

It beckoned me, it pulled me. The grass and moss were dewy beneath my feet, though I felt them not. The wind was chilly on my skin, though I did not notice it. Distantly I thought I heard Inge call for me. Step by step, I made my way to the Lake: walking, and then wading, into its dark depths.

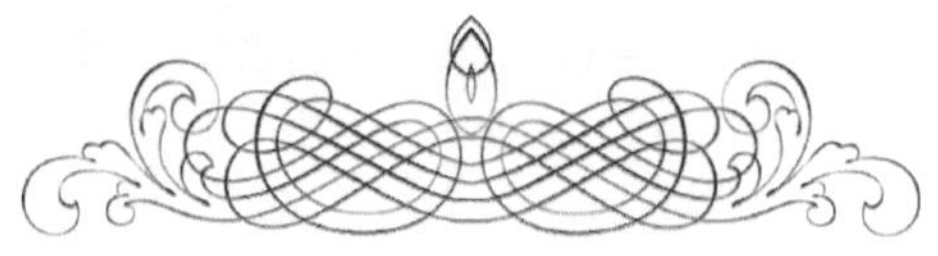

*S*ISTER. *SISTER.*

A *spädba* was crying, awake, and wailing in a wooden cradle. No, not *spädba*. This was something different. This was not a being that had lived through many lives. This being felt too new and too different. This being was too familiar. I walked up to the cradle to see it: a lohyue child. and tried to touch whatever this being was. Soft steps echoed behind me.

Six lohyues entered the room, ignoring me entirely.

"Where am I, who are you?" My words echoed from the stone walls.

They paid me no mind.

"Dear child, you shall serve us as no one else has. A saint you shall be."

They lifted this child from the cradle, and wrapped it tightly in a sheer but coarse fabric, swaddling it so tightly that I wondered if the infant could still breathe. I followed them down damp corridors, descended through dark stairwells until we left the callous castle and were outside. Though I could not feel it, there was a breeze that would have been familiar. I somehow knew it was there, though. I should remember this place, this different time and space.

The dew of midnight, the diamond stars in a different lake. They did not have a care for their long flowing robes as they walked into this lake, one of them clutching the infant closely to their chest. They dipped this child, infant, into the water and what cries the child had made on the way here were silenced. The child quieted, these humans said words that felt as though they should be familiar. Words I should remember. It was a prayer of sorts, though to what or who I could not guess. Whispers and echoes that chaffed my skin.

Then they dropped the newborn, and letting it sink into the depths of this lake, the moon which had been so bright in the sky was now obscured by a sudden storm of clouds. No illumination for a drowning child to reach for.

The Lake of the Mirror births us, and Lake of the Mirror welcomes us back when our time comes again to go back to the spirit world and wait for our next rebirth. But not like this, not like this. This was something different. To humans, this was not a ceremony: it was death.

"No!" The six humans lingered in the lake, their blue robes and long veils moving with the ripples. Then they walked away. "No! Come back! Come back!"

When they did not respond, I ran into the lake. The water moved through me instead of around. Still, I swam as fast as I could and then dove into the darkness. I could find this infant; I could save them. I could save them. I could. I could. I would.

*S*ISTER. *SISTER.*

The courtyard was still, silent. But full of some energy, some presence I could not describe. It pressed in on me and made me feel out of space, the other side of what was happening to Adrian. My ahn-hörn felt too heavy now, too warm. Only ever had it been cold: a cruel and constant reminder. Now it was a weight, now it was an ember. The obsidian matching the dark of the night too perfectly. Reflecting starlight back to the sky, an eerie orange glow. It resonated, but I could not tell with what.

Quiet as silk in the wind, a lohyue entered the courtyard, and another followed behind. The second made not even the ghost of a sound, far too quiet to be real. But both figures felt familiar. As they moved from the shadow into the illuminated center, I realized I did recognize one of them. Ylve. Wearing the clothing of a lohyue, hood pulled low to hide their *Ástfríður* features, *ahnhörn* absent.

"Sister," Ylve said. "She will be at the lake, as you promised?" *Sister*. The words ricocheted through me, a physical shaking of my being.

"Yes, she will be. As your *spädba* will arrive at ours. Here." The lohyue held out their hands, cupping what had to be a metal ore. "When the time is right, use this."

A metal ore, though I could not see it, I thought I should be able to identify it. I was a broken Ástfríður, so the power to feel it was not in me. Still. I should know it. Still, I could feel it. A whisper on the wind, and then gone again.

The two of them clasped hands around this ore, and the lohyue muttered some words, speaking them to the moon. The words moved through my head, danced at the edge of memory. Words that reverberated in my head, pounding like drums.

"Thank you, Sister," Ylve said, pocketing the ore. "I am glad we could make such an arrangement." Ylve turned their back on this lohyue and quickly tried to make their exit.

"Ylve. Your greed proceeds you."

They turned back on their heel and slowly approached the lohyue again; displaying an aggression and anger I had never seen in them before. "And what of yours, Sister? The Araelta gain what, exactly, from this exchange? Are you not also benefiting from our deal? Did you not also want something from me?"

"Our mission is more than what you might be able to comprehend. But yours? Selfish. Limited only to your personal gain."

"You seek to win a petty and needless war that has spanned centuries." Though Ylve was whispering, I could tell they wanted to shout. They emphasized each word, their finger jabbing into the Sister's chest. "We are not so different, I think. We can all justify ourselves, sleep at night believing we are doing what is right. Who is more aware of it, though?"

"You know nothing of our war and nothing of what is at stake. Not of the Blodheimr Hjart, nor the new gods." The Sister spoke quietly, calmly, unimpressed and unmoved by Ylve's words.

"And you know nothing of what will become of the *Ástfríður* if I fail here."

*S*ISTER. *SISTER.*

Water filled my lungs, stinging, unending, relentless. Screams died in my throat, I thrashed in vain. In every direction was endless darkness. There was no light that I could find, no hints of a surface. Just dark waters. The dark waters that the infant had been drowned in. The dark waters I had been born from. Endless, timeless. Miles away, the two lakes. But right now, they felt as one. My heart trying to find the child. My mind trying to find the way back to Inge.

Sister. Sister. Come back to us. False ones stole you, false ones discarded you.

I saw the infant, in the distance. Cradled by the moon, the stars reaching out, seeking her. The waters wanting to care for her. But she was not moving, still and silent. I swam. I could save her yet.

Sister. Sister. Sister. Sister. Sister. Astrid, named of the stars you were made from, cared for by the waters. As all of the Sisters are.

Water rushed by me, through me, as I pushed it aside, and made my way to the child. I grabbed her; she was just as light and as incorporeal as myself. I could save her; I could save her. We floated in moonlight, suspended in night-shaded lake. But then she stirred and I rubbed my *ahnhörn* against her cheek, a gesture of safety, a promise of protection.

I was disposable to them. I had no value outside of a bargaining chip. Ylve did not love me, the Araelta did not love me. I belonged nowhere. I was discarded, and I was stolen. I was not enough to belong anywhere. They said I was to serve them in ways greater than anyone else in the order had, to give them power. I was not enough for them to think of me as anything but the price of power in a war. I was not enough.

Somewhere, in Fayn, somewhere in the temples of these Seekers, there lived an *Ástfríður*. The one who should have appeared at the Lake. I was not enough. I had no value to them as an individual, as myself.

The Araelta gave me away, but Ylve only took me for their own reasons. For some personal, self-serving reason. Raised me only for selfish reasons, for some power that I did not want to guess at. I was not a beloved charge; whatever they did to hide me from the rest of the clan was not because they loved me, not because they could not bear to see me cast out. I was kept here because they needed me for their own devices, and not because they saw me as a being, whole and worthy. I was not enough for them, either. Deep inside I knew that nothing had changed over the years, and they had not come to love me anyway as the years went on. *No one else could love you.*

"Astrid! Astrid, please."

Sister.

"Astrid, can you hear me? Please. It's Inge, please come back. Please."

Sister.

"Astrid...I can't...I can't lose you, come back! Come back."

The moon and the stars and the water vanished in a flood of darkness.

"Astrid!"

THERE IS A MOMENT between waking and sleeping where you are nowhere. The moment before you open your eyes. The moment when the world around you seems out of place, unreal. Trapped in that moment, I was not sure if I wanted to stay there or open my eyes. Face what it was that I had to face. Accept what I had to accept.

"Astrid!"

I could not face this. I would stay here, this hazy world of nothing, this world where I can drown in dreams. Flee from the endless nightmare that was my reality. Drifting in oblivion.

"Astrid! Stay with me now, stay with me. Please. Stay."

Inge.

"Astrid! Please stay with me now. You are safe, you are safe."

Inge. No, it was a lie.

"Astrid, I can't lose you. Please. I need you!"

They do not know, if they did... I will never be enough for Inge...For Inge. And yet. "I am here."

Inge had pulled me to the shore, back to the edge of the Lake. Had wrapped their arms around me and held me tightly. Had wanted me. Me. They said they could not lose me, and it felt as though it had nothing to do with my ability to help Adrian and everything to do with me.

"Oh my gosh. Oh, love. I was so worried. You walked into the Lake and then..."

My knees refused to support me as I tried to stand. I could barely manage to sit up. I noticed the weight of my ahnhörn was gone from my head, and saw it floating at the center of the Lake. It was beautiful, the obsidian caught the light of the stars and it glowed. Ylve. The ore given to them.

A spell of binding, an exchange. I did not want to think more on that, I did not want to follow those thoughts down the road, to whatever truths were at the end of it. The heat of the copper necklace on my chest, the copper that Ylve chose for themself so many decades before I was given as their charge. "You said I could help Adrian."

"I believe so."

"Why?" I looked at the stars, and at the *ahnhörn;* into the distance, into the water.

"There is something that feels wrong with them. And when I saw you...There was something running through you. Metal magic... but flowing differently than anyone else's. Mixed up, more than just obsidian. Part silver, and part copper, too. I thought maybe you had chosen differently. Had your own reasons for wanting obsidian in this life. But never broken, I never thought that you were broken, or wrong. But then you said you couldn't feel it..."

"I do not have metal magic. I am not *Ástfríður*." The words should have stung, words that I had been unknowingly fighting to both say and not know my whole life. I spoken them calmly, monotone. But said them, nonetheless.

"What are you, Astrid? If not *Ástfríður*?"

The only one who could love you...

"A pawn. Inge, were there any others who were wanted to participate in the *väljasång*?"

"Four were called, though I Scryed five…"

Silver. Copper. Adrian. Ylve. "You need to destroy this." I removed the copper necklace, wanting to hold it tightly for comfort, as I had so many times before, and handed it to Inge. "And I need you to destroy that, too." I pointed to the center of the Lake, the black hole that had seemed to take form there.

"It's sacrilege. Astrid, why?"

"I know it is against our beliefs. But, please." I knew, somehow, that doing so would stop whatever was flowing through my body, but I was not sure if that would kill me. Silver flowing through me, to take root in copper. And we…they, *Ástfríður*…are nothing without the magic that flows within, the metal that they choose to house their soul. I had been born cursed to be a vessel for the magic. More hollow than I could imagine.

"What!? Why?"

"You said you thought I could help Adrian. They are the next *sång*. Please. Do it." Inge nodded, understanding on their face, determined.

Dying stars expand, and then fly apart into infinitely small pieces, to be reborn. To become new stars.

T HE HEALERS COULD DO nothing for Ylve; they remained unconscious, unmoving. Inge had carried me out of the forest and was immediately beset upon by half the village calling for them, calling for me. Ylve had collapsed, screaming my name before they fell unconscious. They wasted away little by little over the following week. All that could be done was try to make them comfortable. The elders expected me to remain by Ylve's side; I wanted anything but that. I could not bear to be near them. But I stayed there, Inge keeping me company at first, and then Adrian, solid and bright and shining Adrian, joined us.

“C HILD...ASTRID...” YLVE SAID A week later. “My wayward, willful charge. Where is your *ahnhörn?*”

Whatever explanation Inge gave to the elders for my *ahnhörn* disappearing, for any of them realizing that suddenly there was no metal flowing through me, they did not tell me. No one questioned Inge. They had covered for me more than Ylve ever had, I realized.

“Gone,” was all that I could say. I clasped my hands together in my lap, my head drooping down.

"Ah. I will need to..." they paused, noticing Inge for the first time. "You will need to make a new one. I shall make it my first priority as *sång*."

"You will not be taking part in that ceremony," Inge stood up from their chair, back straight, eyes full of gold. "I have foreseen the next *sång*. There is no need for that ceremony."

Ylve stayed silent.

"Adrian will be *sång* as soon as the current one goes through *väljanda* and rejoins the spirits to await their next birth. But that is a long ways off, yet."

Bright, silver shining Adrian.

"STAY. PLEASE. STAY," INGE said, coming from nowhere as she had so silently slipped in.

"I do not belong here. I am not a child of the Lake," I said, placing just a few trinkets into a bag. I wanted to take some of the metal gifts I had been given, trinkets or my favorite mug or jewelry I wore at ceremonies, a small pewter wren and the gold cage I had placed it in. But metal is sacred and should never leave the Veil. I was lohyue, though I could not break the traditions I had been raised in, could not simply discard all I had been taught, could not suddenly turn away from beliefs I still held. The Veil was special, there was something in the Veil that existed nowhere else, something powerful. This was a belief, more than a belief, I always would hold; that would never change. I did not want to change. Though sometimes I wondered if I should, if it would be easier that way.

There was no road for me to even see, no road that I could walk on. There was no path that could lead me to somewhere I truly belonged. Though the stars claimed me, the temple that worshipped them did not.

I could wander Fayn, the nearest of the outside world; leave the Veil and take up residence in a lohyue city, I had been born in one of them, after all. Sometimes *Ástfriður* would leave the Veil for a while, to learn or to study, or even for leisure. They always returned, though. If they could find their way out there, I could, too. They always returned, never able to make it their home. Though I was *Ástfriður* raised, these outside lands were where I must go. I would never truly belong there, though, either.

"You belong with me, though. Please, Astrid. You belong with me."

"Inge, no. I am lohyue, a lohyue blessed by the stars. But a lohyue. A lohyue can never be good enough for the Scryer of the Mirror of the Lake. And a lohyue does not belong in the Veil."

Inge pulled a band of gold from their pouch, a beautiful and intricate bracelet, and held it out to me. "Will you?" they asked.

A bracelet of partnership. A promise. A declaration of love. A spiritual place of belonging. Permission to live here, to stay.

"I am not good enough for this, Inge."

"Astrid, stay with me. Please."

"I am not..."

Inge closed the gap between us, pressed the bracelet against my chest with both of their hands, and looked me in the eye, more than one question on their lips. "I have seen you; I have seen all of you. Don't you see? I love you. I will continue to love you; I am far from having loved you enough."

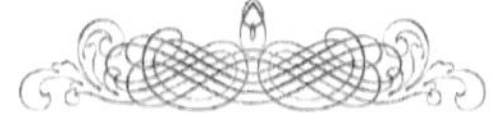

Thank you for taking the time to read *Shades and Silver*. I wrote these stories for many reasons, one among them being my love of unicorns. But I also wrote these stories to explore what disability might look like in a world where one's worth was not defined necessarily by one's labor or job title, how one might still struggle with feelings of being burdensome or worthless. As an indie author, I rely on reviews to make sure my books find their way into the hands of readers who need them. It would be a great help to me and others searching for books like *Shades and Silver* if you left an honest <u>review</u>. It doesn't need to be much, just two or three sentences. Thank you from the bottom of my heart.

The Ástfríður

Average Lifespan: Unknown

Diet: Unknown

Age of Maturity: Unknown

Their Culture:

The Ástfríður has a deep connection with the earth and
its resources. They possess the unique ability to sense
the presence of metals within the ground, allowing

them to locate and summon these metals to the surface. However, rather than exploiting these resources for personal gain, the Ástfríður view metal as sacred and precious. They believe that the gods have bestowed upon them the responsibility to protect and honor these divine gifts.

In their worship of the gods, the Ástfríður channel their skills and creativity into crafting intricate metal artworks. These masterpieces serve as offerings and symbols of devotion, reflecting their reverence for the gods. Metal is seen not only as a material for construction or weaponry, but as a medium of spiritual expression.

In order to maintain their connection with the divine and to respect the gods' will, the Ástfríður refrain from building their homes using metal. They believe dwelling in a metal structure would be an act of arrogance, as it implies an attempt to rival the gods' creation.

Instead, they coexist peacefully in the forest's depths, surrounded by beauty and abundance.

The Ástfríður have distanced themselves from Lohyue and Qatu-Calla civilizations, as they perceive both species to be wasteful with metal, often using it for destructive purposes such as warfare and excessive construction. They view such actions as disrespectful to the gods and the sacredness of metal. By isolating themselves in the forest, the Ástfríður strive to preserve the purity of their beliefs and to protect the sanctity of metal from Lohyue greed and exploitation.

Reincarnation:

The Ástfríður believe in reincarnation as a sacred form of reproduction. When they sense the beckoning to return to the earth, they embark on a pilgrimage, each one drawn by the veins of the earth to a distinct location. They never disclose their chosen destination to others. In due time, a späda Ástfríður will be discovered at the base of the clan's sacred tree, with the same complexion as their previous life and adorned with a bracelet crafted from their previous ahnhörn.

The more conservative members of the Ástfríður keep this tree nestled inside their revered temple, whereas the more liberal ones locate it at the heart of their bustling village. Sometimes, individuals from one clan will reincarnate into the other, blurring the boundaries between their communities. Even exiles, who had long departed from the clan, have been found at the tree's base decades after their departure. These foundlings, often resembling three-year-old human children in size, bear bracelets large enough to fit an adult wrist. Although they lack memories of their past lives, they are often regaled with tales from those who were present during their previous existence. They relinquish their former names, embracing the belief that each life should have its distinct identity.

In these cases, the Ástfríður meticulously plans their demise in a manner that conceals their true intentions. The gods, who hold the power over life and death, are aware of these occurrences and often choose to intervene in extraordinary circumstances.

Väljahnhörn - Choosing their metals:

During the Väljahnhörn ceremony, each individual selects a specific metal to represent their identity. These metals serve as both symbolic adornments and manifestations of their unique attributes and values. They may choose any metal, including gold, silver, copper, bronze, iron, etc. As they craft their chosen metal into an ahnhörn, they infuse it with their own personal energy and magic, ensuring that it reflects their inner self. The ahnhörn becomes an integral part of their identity, serving as a visible symbol of their values.

Moreover, the metals can be combined in various ways, such as spiraling two or three together, representing fluidity and the intersection of multiple values and paths. Individuals can also choose to melt metals together, creating alloys that embody a blending of values.

The Ástfríður have the custom of touching their ahnhörns together as a respectful and welcoming gesture, acknowledging each other's chosen path.

Notable Clans:

The Lake of the Mirror: A clan that values dance

Mountain-at-Dawn: A more conservative clan that does not believe that forging metal should be done for decorative or recreational items.

Valley-at-Dusk: A clan that values knowledge and are extremely secretive; even other clans do not know much about these reclusive people.

Language:

Isjälsfrä: A rare phenomenon where two souls meet multiple times throughout all of their reincarnations. Some do not believe this exists.

Tvära: One who is born into a clan has no previous

history within the reincarnation cycle.

Tonå: An Ástfríður who has not completed their coming-of-age ceremony.

Spädba: The equivalent of an infant.

Klämta: The bell that rings when a Spädba is found.

The Sång: The leader of a clan.

Ahnhörn: The circlet and horn that an Ástfríður forges for themselves.

Väljahnhörn: The coming-of-age ritual in which and Ástfríður chooses which metal they will identify with.

Ahnhörnu: An Ástfríður who has completed their coming-of-age ceremony and chosen their metal. An adult in the clan with rights and responsibilities.

Aserphodels.: The Place of Rebirth. Unique for each individual. It is here that the souls of these people are absorbed back into the aclaere to be reborn.

Aclaere: The life-force of the planet.

WITH MANY THANKS TO Jan Anderson of Clearing Blocks Editing for helping tie this together and polish my vision. Thank you to Merilliza Chan for the gorgeous illustration for the cover. Thank you to my cats, too. They spent many hours sitting on the keyboard despite my attempts to keep them off of it, they claim they had some inspiration to add.

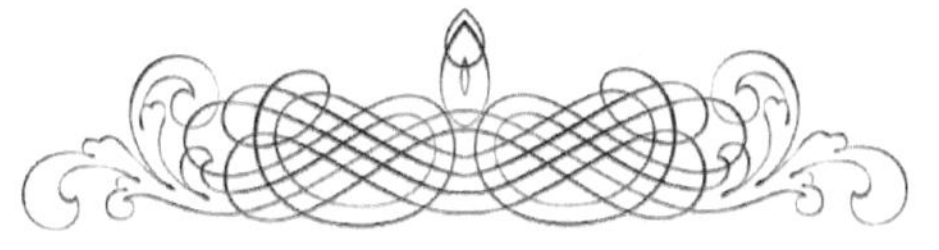

The Magic Surrendered

A Lake of Feathers and Moonbeams

Birthing Orion

Scions and Shadows:

Shades and Silver

Stars and Soil

Coming Soon: Smoke and Steel

daxmurray.com

@daxaeterna

Sign up for Dax's newsletter at https://www.daxmur ray.com/newsletter for twice-monthly updates and an early peek at her current WIP, discounts for the store, plus other goodies.

Use discount code **DREAMER** for a free month on Dax's Ream Membership at the ENCHANTER tier, where you will have unlimited access to Dax's backlist, plus Ream Exclusive serials, short stories, and bonus materials.

https://subscribe.daxmurray.com

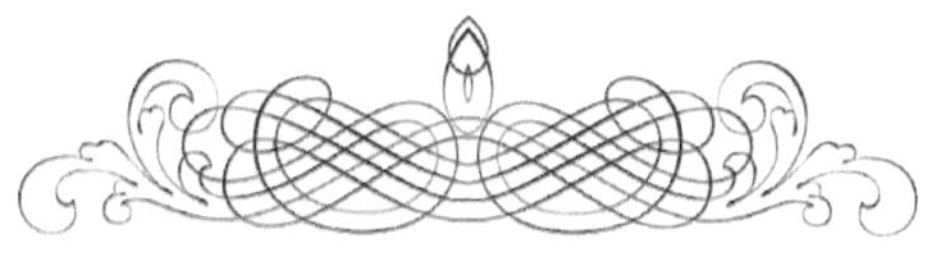

D AX WRITES WITH THE Kraken Collective, an alliance of indie authors of LGBTQIAP+ speculative fiction. If you enjoyed After Images you may also enjoy:

Moon-Bright Tides by RoAnna Sylver

The night sky is very dark without a moon, and there hasn't been one for decades. Without one to govern the oceans, it falls to Riven, reluctant sea-witch, to sail out alone every night across the midnight ocean to cast a spell to call in the tides.

She hates it. Hates the moonless dark, hates the endless deep, and hates the fact that without a witch to sing in the tides, sea and land alike would fall to ruin. Riven faces her worst fear every night for years – until she meets a mermaid. Her new friend is lost, starving, and just as lonely as she is. And now that they've found one another, neither of their nights on the midnight sea will be the same.

Copyright 2021 by Dax Murray

First edition, January 2021

Cover illustration by Merilliza Chan

Edited by Jan Anderson, Clearing Blocks Editing

Interior Design by Dax Murray

Published by the Kraken Collective

Copyright 2021 by Dax Murray

Published with The Kraken Collective